WITH BELLS ON

A CHRISTMAS STORY

Story and Pictures by KATHERINE MILHOUS

CHARLES SCRIBNER'S SONS

New York

A Note to the Reader

This story takes place in Pennsylvania, a good many years ago. Then people and goods travelled by the big Conestoga wagons made in the Conestoga Valley. Strong Pennsylvania horses pulled the wagons along the rough roads and over the steep mountain ranges— where now cars go swiftly along the smooth Turnpike.

Many Christmas customs were brought from the countries across the sea—you will find some of them in this story. At Christmas time it was not Santa Claus but the Christ Child who brought gifts. He came riding on a donkey. Then too, in many homes there was the making of the "putz," or Christmas manger scene.

After you have read the book and looked at the pictures, you may want to make a "putz" of your own. Make it in your own way, with the materials that you have, for there are other materials than those these country children found. You may want to use cardboard or wood for the stable, clay to make the people. Green cloth will do instead of moss, but be sure to use some Christmas greens to make it look like the outdoors. And when you have made a really beautiful "putz" you will want to invite your friends in to see it.

JONATHAN was going away and Chrissly and Becky had got up by candlelight to see him off. They would miss their brother very much. Jonathan said good-bye to Mother and Grandpa and then all three set out on their walk through the woods.

It was scary going through the woods in the dark. Becky held tightly to Jonathan's hand, but Chrissly walked alone, lifting the lantern high so that they would not trip over dead logs and fallen branches. They walked softly over the soggy leaves. All above and below and around them they heard the small sounds made by small creatures as they fled, frightened, from the light of the lantern.

"Hurry!" said Jonathan. "If I'm late, Uncle will leave without me. He wants me to help with the horses, you know."

When they reached the edge of the woods, they saw the great white-topped Conestoga wagon standing by the roadside. Uncle Ned was already sitting astride the saddle horse. The six sturdy horses stood patiently, their collars adorned with hoops of bells and with colored ribbons and dangling tassels.

"Jon," said Becky. "Promise you'll be home for Christmas."

"I promise," said Jonathan. "But you two will have to make the Christmas putz. Promise?"

"We promise! We promise!"

Jonathan climbed up on the wagon seat. Uncle cracked the whip. The horses strained. They were off—with a jingle, jangle—and a jinglety, janglety, jang!

"I'll be home for Christmas," Jonathan shouted above the jangle. "I'll be home—with bells on!"

FINDING THE MOSS AND STUMPS

Chrissly and Becky hurried home. Mother needed help with the housework and Grandpa needed help around the barn. Father had died when the children were very small and since then Grandpa had kept the farm going.

That evening Chrissly and Becky remembered their promise to Jon. Could *they* make a putz? Jon had made one each year—just a small Christmas crib with the Holy Family and the animals on a pile of straw. Then he had banked evergreens behind it and lighted candles before it. It was lovely!

They found the putz figures in the stair closet. There were Mary, Joseph and the baby Jesus—Grandpa had carved those. And there were the ox and the donkey that Jon had carved.

"Jon wanted to make a stable for the Holy Family," said Chrissly, "but now he's gone away. I'll make the stable myself. And won't Jon be surprised!"

The little figures were beautiful in the glow of the fireplace. Mother and Grandpa got to talking about the wonderful putzes of the old days—putzes so large that they filled all one end of a room.

"Oh, let's make a BIG putz for Jon," said Becky. "I'll make the Star in the East."

"And remember there were Wise Men who followed the star," said Grandpa, "and shepherds who watched their flocks by night."

"And don't forget," said Mother. "There were angels . . ."

"Oh, I'll make the shepherds and Wise Men and ang—" But Becky saw that everyone was smiling at her promises.

"Well," said Grandpa, "if you want to make a BIG putz, the first thing you do is to go to the woods and get a whole lot of moss and tree bark and old stumps."

THEN THE GREENS AND HOLLY

Chrissly and Becky gathered the moss in the autumn woods. They put the moss down in the cellar and sprinkled it to keep it fresh. Chrissly brought the bark and stumps home in a wheelbarrow. The woods were full of brown mushrooms and the trees were alive with chirping brown birds. Only the glossy green Christmas fern reminded them that Christmas was coming.

Then the weather grew cold and the sky turned gray.

"Now is the time to get the greens and holly for the putz," said Grandpa.

So Chrissly and Becky went again to the woods and gathered all the evergreens and holly they could carry. On their way home great wet snowflakes began to whirl through the air.

"Such big snowflakes!" said Mother, as she opened the kitchen door. "When it snows like this, they say our neighbors over the hills are plucking their geese!" Suddenly Christmas seemed very near.

That evening Chrissly looked up from the stable he was making and said, "Grandpa, where do you think Jon is tonight?"

"Nearing Philadelphia, maybe." Grandfather knew the Conestoga wagon trail well. As a young man he had owned and driven a Conestoga wagon himself. What a sight it was to see thousands of wagons pass along the trail in a single day! Grandpa went to the window and stood looking out into the storm.

"But the wagons didn't always pass," he said. "Sometimes a wagoner would get stuck in mud or snow. Then, if another wagoner pulled him out, he had to give that fellow his bells as a reward."

"Why," said Chrissly, "that's what Jon meant when he said he'd be home for Christmas—with bells on!"

THEN TO THE STORE

The big flakes kept coming down. Chrissly worked on his stable and Becky watered the greens in the cellar. They missed Jonathan more and more every day.

The cellar was cold and Becky wished that she had never promised to make the shepherds and the Wise Men and the angels for the putz. However could she make them? Christmas was coming nearer and nearer, and what had she made so far? Only the Star in the East that she had covered with tinfoil from a teabox. You couldn't make a BIG putz with just one star.

Mother said it was time to bake the Christmas cookies. When the snow stopped, she called to Chrissly, "Get the sled and go to the village. Tell Mr. Greensleeves I need flour, sugar, and spices. Yes, Becky, you may go too." She gave them each some pennies to spend.

Chrissly spent his pennies for candy, but Becky was looking for something very special. The shop was gaily decorated for Christmas with garlands and wreaths, and the window was full of toys and games and books. But these were not things you could use in a putz.

"Oh, Mr. Greensleeves," said Becky, "don't you have any Wise Men for sale?"

"How's that?" asked the storekeeper, leaning across the counter.

"Or any shepherds or angels?" said Becky. But before he could answer, she said, "I'll take those little white penny dolls."

When she got home, she dyed the tiny dolls with beet juice. Then she pasted paper wings on them. What lovely pink angels they made!

THE PEDDLER COMES

But you couldn't make a BIG putz with a few pink angels and a star. And Becky did want to have a wonderful putz as a surprise for Jon.

It began to snow again—this time the snow was fine and drifting. Soon everything was white as far as you could see, which wasn't far, at all. Grandpa and Chrissly had to shovel a path to the barn to reach the hungry cattle. Becky helped Mother bake the Christmas cookies. Katze, the kitten, slept contentedly before the fireplace.

It snowed for three days. "The peddler will never get through in this weather," said Grandpa. When Becky heard that she could have cried. Her toy bank rattled with pennies. She had hoped the peddler would have some little figures she could buy for the putz.

But the peddler did come! "Don't I always come for Christmas?" he asked with a grin. He had come in a sleigh instead of in his usual wagon. He carried a tray loaded with gaily painted plaster ornaments—birds and animals and little people and castles. Mother bought all sorts of cookie cutters. But on the peddler's tray there were no shepherds or Wise Men.

That evening Mother looked as if she had been crying. Almost in a whisper she said, "I wonder where Jon is now."

"If they have sold all their goods," said Grandpa, "they left the city several days ago. Better if they haven't, for the mountain roads are dangerous in a storm. Listen to that wind. Trees blow down, there are landslides, and . . ."

"Just the same, Jon will get through," said Chrissly. "I know he will."

MAKING THE PUTZ FIGURES

Now they were really snowed in. The moss and the evergreens for the BIG putz still lay in the cellar. But how could Becky make the shepherds and the Wise Men? She couldn't carve, she hadn't even a paint-box.

Maybe Mother could help. Mother listened, then suddenly put down her mending. She hurried up to the attic and came back carrying two old hatboxes. She ripped the hatboxes apart and flattened them out. Then she began to sketch quickly on the cardboard which was covered with colored wallpaper. Becky and Chrissly watched as she drew the outlines of shepherds and sheep and Wise Men.

"It's been a long time," said Mother, laughing, "since I drew a line, except in someone's album. But I used to be very good at drawing when I went to school. We had the biggest putz anywhere around. We even had tiny villages under the evergreens and lots of little village people bringing their gifts to the manger."

Mother went on to draw some of the little people—an old woman with a basket of eggs, a fiddler, a farmer, a blacksmith, a miller, and many others.

"Now, Becky," she said, "take the scissors and cut these out."

Katze began madly rolling a ball of wool across the room. "Bless your heart, Katze!" said Mother. "You've given me an idea."

Mother took several of the figures that Becky had cut out.

"Now we'll dress them up," she said. With bits of bright colored wool she embroidered designs on the robes and crowns of the Wise Men and she wound white wool around the bodies of the sheep.

THE CHRISTMAS ROSE

When they were finished, the cardboard figures were really beautiful. Becky found that she, too, could sew with the colored wool, and in a few days she finished all the little people that Mother had drawn. Chrissly built tiny houses, and a church and a schoolhouse. On the day before Christmas, with Grandpa's help, they set up the putz.

Twilight came—the twilight of Christmas Eve. But Jonathan did not come with the twilight. The snow had stopped and they listened for the crunch of his boots on the snow crust. Beneath the pear tree the Christmas rose was blooming. Surely, if a rose could bloom in the snow, Jonathan could come safely through the storm.

Before dark, Mother put some of the bread she had baked on the window sill. In the morning she would break the bread, wet with the Christmas dew, and give a piece to each member of the family to eat. There would then be health and happiness in the family all year long.

Grandfather went to the barn and raked a pile of hay into the barnyard. The Christkind—the Christchild—would be coming at midnight and there must be hay for his donkey. In the morning the cattle would munch the blessed hay and grow fat and sleek.

Then Grandfather bound straw around the trunks of all the fruit trees. He knelt by the pear tree beneath which the Christmas rose was blooming and spoke to the tree.

"On this night is born our Lord.
You, O Tree, His love reward.
With this straw I wrap you round,
That your fruit may reach the ground."

CHRISTMAS EVE

Darkness came—the darkness of Christmas Eve. The lamp was trimmed and lighted. The cookies were baked, the bread was on the window sill, the hay piled in the barnyard, the fruit trees bound with straw. The putz was ready. They were all waiting—waiting for Jonathan.

Because it was Christmas Eve, Mother said they would dress up in their Sunday best. They sat quietly around the table under the lamp. Hoping to cheer them, Mother brought plates of cookies and told Chrissly to pop corn in the fireplace.

"With bells on! With bells on!" Chrissly said over and over as he shook the corn popper.

"Stop, Chrissly!" said Grandpa. "Listen!" They listened while the sound came nearer and nearer. BELLS! They all ran to the door—but it was only a passing sleigh. After that, the hands of the old clock on the mantel seemed to stand still.

Grandfather held the family Bible on his knees, but his thoughts were far away along the Conestoga wagon trail.

Mother mended her shawl from time to time, but mostly it lay in her lap. She could think only of Jonathan, lost somewhere in the night and the snow.

Chrissly sat holding his ship, his favorite plaything. Jon had made it for him.

Becky tried to play with Katze, rolling a ball of wool right under the kitten's nose. But Katze wouldn't play.

Grandpa began to read them the Christmas story. When he came to the verse, "And the angel said unto them, 'Fear not—'" he stopped and said a prayer for Jonathan.

"Becky! Chrissly! You must go to bed now," said Mother.

"But Jon! We want to wait up for Jon!" said Becky.

Chrissly looked at the clock. "It's almost Christmas now," he said. "Can't we stay up a little longer?"

"No!" said Mother. "The Christkind comes at midnight. If you're not in bed he won't stop and leave your presents. We'll wait up, Grandpa and I."

"I don't think Jon will come tonight," said Grandpa. "It's a hard thing to go through the woods on a winter's night. Besides, even if all is well, the teamsters may be snowed in, spending the night in some tavern along the way and resting the horses." Grandpa spoke cheerfully but he looked worried.

"But Jon promised he'd be home—and with bells on," said Chrissly.

"This is Jon's first trip. He didn't know what it means to be a wagoner. Now off to bed with you," said Grandpa sternly.

Chrissly and Becky undressed before the fireplace. They put their nightgowns on over their underwear, for it was bitter cold in the attic room where they slept. They started up the stairs, Chrissly carrying the candle and a hot brick covered with newspaper to keep his feet warm. Becky wrapped herself in Mother's old shawl to use as an extra blanket. She carried Katze, who would sleep at her feet. Katze was better than a brick because she didn't cool off all night long.

When they were halfway up the stairs, Becky whispered, "Chris, let's go down and look at the putz again. Maybe Jon will come while we're in the parlor."

THE WONDERFUL PUTZ

The putz filled all one corner of the parlor. By candlelight it looked dark and mysterious. There were hills and valleys made of moss-covered stumps and tree bark, and the green landscape was dotted all over with tiny evergreen trees.

A road wound down to the stable where the baby Jesus lay in the manger with Mary and Joseph beside Him. Chrissly had made the stable just like their own barn. He had even made the painted decorations and the stalls for Hossasock, the horse, and Gus, the ox. Shepherds led their sheep up to the manger and the Wise Men came with their gifts of gold, frankincense and myrrh.

Down the road came the country folk—country folk like their own neighbors. It was as if Mr. Greensleeves came with his toys, Mrs. Stolz, the washerwoman, with clean linen, Farmer Jones with a bundle of hay, Granny Wilkins with a basket of eggs and a can of milk, Miller Heller with a sack of flour. Down the road, too, came a Conestoga wagon—a tiny six-horse bell team. One could almost hear the bells go jingle, jangle.

Becky's pink angels hung from the ceiling, gently swinging and swaying in the draft from the window. High above, in the heaven of the putz, shone the star of Bethlehem with its rays of white wool.

Cold as it was in the parlor, they stood for a long time before the putz. Then a wonderful thing happened! In the candlelight the putz no longer looked small. It was no longer something they had made themselves. It was real! It was the Christmas story come to life.

Quietly they closed the parlor doors and went up to bed.

IN THE ATTIC

Chrissly and Becky slept on opposite sides of the attic. There was a small window beside each bed. Becky's window looked over the barnyard and Chrissly's over the hills and the valleys. A bright moon lighted the window panes. The attic smelled of apples and the dried herbs that hung from the low beams.

"Chris, come away from that window," said Becky. "The Christkind won't come if you're looking for him."

"I was looking for Jon," said Chrissly "But I don't see anything but white. The whole world is white. Jon promised . . ."

"Get in bed, Chris," said Becky. For comfort she stroked Katze who purred contentedly.

Chrissly got under the covers but he couldn't go to sleep. Pictures kept coming into his mind, and, for the first time, he was afraid for Jonathan.

"Becky," he said, "I can see the wagon, tiny—tiny. And I can see the mountains, high—high. The wagon is coming along the edge of a cliff. The night is all black and the snow is coming down and . . ."

"It's not, at all." said Becky. "There's a big moon out."

In a few minutes she fell asleep to Katze's lullaby. She dreamed of the Christkind traveling on his donkey all over the world. The Christkind carried a lantern like their barn lantern. Wherever he went, the roads and mountain passes and the trees by the wayside lighted up, but the light did not come from the lantern. It seemed to be shining around his head.

If Jon and the bell team followed the light they would surely come safely home.

THE CHRISTKIND

Now the Christkind was coming through the sleeping village. Now he was coming through the woods. And now—now—he was riding toward the barn. There! He had stopped in the barnyard—a small curly-haired child riding a gentle donkey. The donkey munched the hay that had been left out for him, the toys on his back jiggling up and down with every mouthful. The Christkind sat patiently waiting. All about him was a rosy glow which lit up the barn and awakened the pigeons.

Then Becky awoke. The grandfather clock on the stairs struck twelve. Suppose Jon had come while she was asleep!

"Chris!" she called. "Chris, wake up. Has Jon come?"

"No," said Chrissly, kicking the brick at his feet. "No, NO!"

"Chris," said Becky, "wouldn't you like to hear what the animals say when they talk on Christmas Eve? What do you suppose Hossasock says to Gus and what do you think Gus says to the cows? I'm sure they talk to the Christkind's donkey, aren't you? Oh, I wish I could hear them talk."

Chrissly didn't answer. He was sitting straight up in bed, listening.

"And wouldn't you like to see the bees come out of their hives and go buzzing about in the snow?" said Becky. "Grandpa says they make a joyful noise unto the Lord—Zzzzz—zzzz—hm—hm—Hmm-mm-mm."

"Keep still, Becky," said Chrissly. "Listen!" He jumped out of bed and ran to the window. He raised the window and stood there, shivering and listening.

"BELLS!" he shouted. "I hear BELLS!"

"I hear them, too," said Becky. The bells were strong and clear. "Jon has come home!"

JONATHAN COMES HOME

They ran down the stairs to open the kitchen door.

And there was Jonathan, sliding over the snow crust in the moonlight. Above his head he carried a hoop of jingling wagon bells. He hurried past them into the house and stood before the fireplace, laughing and shaking the bells so that their chimes filled the whole place.

Grandpa took the bells and put them on the mantelpiece. Mother brought food and cookies. Chrissly piled logs on the fire and Becky took Jon's coat and muffler. Katze rubbed against his legs. Oh, it was good to have Jon home again!

"How do you think I got that hoop of bells?" said Jon. "Well, when the big snow hit us we were on a narrow mountain road on the edge of a cliff. The road was full of ruts and rocks and the horses kept slipping. We couldn't see where we were going. The wind was so strong that the horses couldn't hear whether Uncle said 'Gee!' or 'Haw!' So I rode the saddle horse and drove the team. Uncle walked beside the lead horse and talked to him and told him we *had* to get home for Christmas.

"And then—the storm got worse. We put planks under the wheels so that they wouldn't freeze to the road. We put bear skins on the horses and we bedded down in the wagon. You should have heard the wolves howl and the foxes scream all night long! In the morning we came upon a team frozen in a snowbank. We dug her out and so —we got her bells."

"So here I am. Back home for Christmas—with bells on!"

CHRISTMAS MORNING

Morning came—Christmas morning. Before daylight Jon and Grandpa were off to the barn.

"Look, Jon," said Grandpa, pointing with his lantern, "the Christmas rose! And look! The cattle have eaten all the hay."

In the barn Jon found the sack of presents he had left there the night before. He had bought the presents in the city with the money he had got by selling his pig bristles to a brushmaker.

He and Grandpa hurried back to the house. Mother was already setting the breakfast table. There were gifts beside each plate and Jon put his presents with the rest—a watchholder for Grandpa, dress goods for Mother, a penknife for Chrissly, a book for Becky. Just then Becky and Chrissly and Katze came running down the stairs.

After they had all eaten the blessed bread, they opened their presents. It was a good Christmas, thought Jon, but something was missing. There was no putz. There couldn't be a putz, not without evergreens, and Grandpa said they had been snowed in.

But why was everyone going into the parlor? That was where the putz had been on the other Christmases. Jon followed them in.

When he saw the putz Jon could not believe his eyes. The miniature landscape glowed and shimmered in the light of many beeswax candles. It was wonderful and beautiful.

They all gathered around the putz while Grandpa read the Christmas story. Then they sang carols, Jon standing with his arms around Becky and Chrissly, hugging them tight.

"Jon," whispered Becky, "kneel down and get close to the putz."

Jonathan knelt down. Why, he wondered? Suddenly he knew.

"Oh," he said, "it all looks real. And the stable is our own barn—with the Holy Family in it."

THEY ALL MADE CHRISTMAS

In the quiet parlor they drew close together, feeling the deep meaning of Christmas. The Wise Men had come to the manger, bearing their gifts of gold, frankincense, and myrrh. These were the things the Wise Men had to offer. But, as Mother said, the Child needed other things even more—bread and milk and linen, and hay for his bed. We, like the Wise Men, can give only of what we have.

And so : Jonathan had whittled the ox and the donkey and brought presents from the city.

Grandpa had carved the Holy Family and kept the farm.

Chrissly had built the stable and the tiny village.

Becky had made the star and the angels, and helped gather the greens.

Mother had baked the bread and cookies and made the little people for the putz.

Katze had given cheerful company and warmed them in bed.

They had *all* made Christmas. So, too, had Mr. Greensleeves, with his window full of toys, and the peddler who drove his sleigh through the snow. So, too, had Gus, the ox, and Hossasock, the horse. And the cows who gave the milk, the hens who laid the eggs, and the bees who made the honey. So, too, had the evergreens in the woods and the Christmas rose blooming in the snow.

They had all given of what they had—and together they had made this wonderful Christmas.

The room was filled with the fragrance of burning candles. Jonathan still knelt before the putz.

"Jon," said Becky, remembering her dream, "you know it was the Christkind who brought you home, safe and sound."

"I know," said Jonathan. "I know."